STEPHEN BUTLER studied at Bath Academy of Art.
He is a freelance illustrator and a tutor in Basic Design at
City and East London College. His previous books for Frances Lincoln
include **Little Bird**, with Saviour Pirotta, and **Henny Penny**, a new version
of the familiar nursery tale, which he both wrote and illustrated.
Stephen Butler lives in South London.

To Rebecca, Joanne, Cheryl, Charlotte, Charlene,
Danielle and Ross, with love

First published in Great Britain in 1994 by
Frances Lincoln Limited, 4 Torriano Mews
Torriano Avenue, London NW5 2RZ

British Library Cataloguing in Publication Data
available on request

ISBN 0-7112-0855-7 hardback
ISBN 0-7112-0856-5 paperback

Printed and bound in Hong Kong

3 5 7 9 8 6 4 2

THE MOUSE AND THE APPLE

STEPHEN BUTLER

FRANCES LINCOLN

One day Mouse saw a lovely ripe apple on the apple tree.
It was red and shiny, and it looked delicious.
Mouse waited for the apple to fall.

Along came Hen.
"Hello, Mouse! What are you doing?"
"I'm waiting for the apple to fall," said Mouse.
"That's a good idea," said Hen hopefully.
"I'll wait with you."

So Mouse and Hen waited for the apple to fall.

Along came Goose.
"Hello, Mouse! Hello, Hen! What are you doing?"
"We're waiting for the apple to fall," said Hen.
"Apples are my favourite," said Goose greedily.
"I'll wait with you."

So Mouse, Hen and Goose waited for the apple to fall.

Along came Goat.
"Hello, Mouse! Hello, Hen! Hello, Goose!
What are you doing?"
"We're waiting for the apple to fall," said Goose.
"I love apples," said Goat hungrily. "I'll wait with you."

So Mouse, Hen, Goose and Goat waited for
the apple to fall.

Along came Cow.
"Hello, Mouse! Hello, Hen! Hello, Goose! Hello, Goat!
What are you doing?"
"We're waiting for the apple to fall," said Goat.
"I was just thinking about apples," said Cow, licking her lips.
"I'll wait with you."

So Mouse, Hen, Goose, Goat and Cow all waited for the apple to fall.

They waited.
And they waited.
And they waited.

Mouse waited patiently, but Cow, Goat, Goose
and Hen soon grew restless. They thought up
ways to make the apple fall.

"I'll fly up and *knock* it down," said Hen, and she ran towards the tree, flapping her wings.

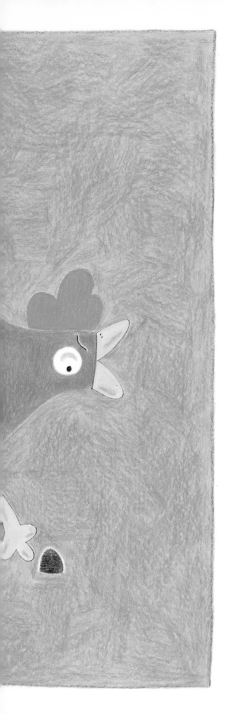

But she tripped, and fell on her beak with a bump.

"I'll *honk* it down," said Goose.
He opened his beak wide. "Honk! Honk! Honk!"

But the apple didn't move.

"I'll *butt* it down," said Goat.
He ran at the tree and butted it as hard as he could.

But the apple didn't budge.

"I've got a good idea!" cried Cow.
She jumped up and down on all four hoofs.

The tree trembled and the apple began to quiver.

"Everybody jump!" cried Cow, jumping up and down.
Goat jumped up and down.
Goose jumped up and down.
Hen jumped up and down.

The tree shook and the apple wobbled,
but still the apple didn't fall.
Meanwhile, Mouse waited patiently.

"Let's go," said Cow grumpily.
"That apple's probably rotten anyway."
"Or sour," said Goat.
"Or hard," said Goose.
"Or soft," said Hen.

Now only Mouse was left.
All of a sudden the shiny red apple
fell to the ground with a plop!

It wasn't rotten or sour or hard or soft.
It was the crunchiest, sweetest,
most delicious apple
Mouse had ever tasted!

MORE YOUNG PAPERBACKS FROM FRANCES LINCOLN

HENNY PENNY
Stephen Butler

When an acorn falls and hits Henny Penny on the head, she thinks the sky is falling. She hurries off to tell the king, and on the way she meets some friends . . . A familiar nursery tale with bright, lively pictures and a surprise ending.
£2.99   ISBN 0-7112-0644-9

LITTLE BIRD
By Saviour Pirotta
Illustrated by Stephen Butler

"What can I do today?" asks the little bird. The bug says *hop*, the worm says *wriggle*, the frog says *jump!* What should Little Bird do? A bold, bright picture book for the very young.
£2.99   ISBN 0-7112-0705-4

HAS ANYONE SEEN JACK?
By Tony Bradman
Illustrated by Margaret Chamberlain

A delightfully cheeky lift-the-flap fairy tale in which naughty Jack gets the better of a comically slow-witted giant.
£3.99   ISBN 0-7112-0728-3

All these books are available at your local bookshop or newsagent, or by post from: Frances Lincoln Paperbacks, P.O. Box 11, Falmouth, Cornwall.

To order, send:
Title, author, ISBN number and price for each book ordered.
Your full name and address.
Cheque or postal order for the total amount, plus postage and packing.
UK: 80p for one book and 20p for each additional book ordered up to a £2.00 maximum.
BFPO: 80p for the first book, plus 20p for each additional book.
Overseas including Eire: £1.60 for the first book, plus £1.00 for the second book, and 30p for each additional book ordered.

Prices and availability subject to change without notice.